Finn's ANIMAL

For Sebastian

First published in Great Britain 1992
by William Heinemann Ltd
Published 1994 by Mammoth
an imprint of Reed International Books Ltd
Michelin House, 81 Fulham Road, London SW3 6RB
and Auckland, Melbourne, Singapore and Toronto

Reprinted 1995 (twice)

Text copyright © Catherine Storr 1992
Illustrations copyright © Paul Howard 1992

The moral right of the author has been asserted

ISBN 0 7497 1644 4

A CIP catalogue record for this title
is available from the British Library

Printed and bound in Great Britain
by Cox & Wyman Ltd, Reading, Berkshire

Finn's ANIMAL

Catherine Storr

Illustrated by Paul Howard

MAMMOTH

Finn and The Animal

"Go up to your room and fetch me your clean trousers, please, Finn. I must sew that button on the waistband before you go to school tomorrow," his mum said one evening.

"I don't need the button," Finn said.

"Of course you do. How can you wear trousers that don't do up properly?" his mum asked.

"I can wear another pair," said Finn.

"You haven't got another pair. Go *on*, Finn, don't hang about."

"You come too," Finn said to his brother.

"He's doing his homework. Don't interrupt him," said Finn's mum.

"He's frightened to go by himself. He's a baby," Locker said.

"I'm not!" Finn said, and to prove it he went out into the passage, and started up the stairs.

But what Locker had said was true. He was frightened.

To reach his room he had to go past open doors into unlit rooms. Caves of darkness. And the cupboard next to the bathroom, where something gurgled and sighed, like a huge beast expecting its next meal. In daylight, Finn might know that it was the hot cylinder which made those noises, but after dark he wasn't so sure.

Once he had flooded his own room with light, he was safe. But only for the moment. As soon as he had found his clean trousers he would have to turn off the light in the bedroom and go downstairs again, leaving the darkness behind him. That meant running downstairs so quickly that his feet nearly missed steps and he had to cling on to the banister rail to prevent himself falling. When he could, he left the door of the kitchen open, so that he could shoot quickly through into the safety of the

warm, bright room, with Mum and
Locker at the table, and the good smell of
toast and sausages and soap powder and
apples which made him feel comforted
and secure.

Some nights when he was in bed, and
his mum had said "Good night" and
closed the door, he could shut his eyes
and go to sleep at once and not wake up
till morning, and that was fine. But there
were other nights when he woke up and
saw the curtains shift, just a little, as if
someone or something was trying to get
in. As the house cooled down at night,
the wicker chair with the red cushion on
its seat would suddenly creak. Then he'd
start wide awake, and strain his eyes to
see if *something* was sitting in the chair,
looking at him, waiting for him to move,

before it leapt at him.

Of course, he couldn't tell people in case they laughed. His mum knew, and she didn't laugh, but even she didn't know how bad it was. "What are you frightened of?" she had asked him more than once. But all he could say was, "I don't know. Something."

Tonight, as he went into his bedroom, he saw it.

It wasn't yet quite dark, but he wanted to dash in and out quickly. He picked up his trousers and turned towards the door, when out of the corner of his eye, he saw something move. Not the curtain in the wind, this time, and the sound he heard wasn't like the peevish wheeze of the basket chair. There was a horrible moment when he thought he would rush out of the room and try to escape; but instead he was somehow brave enough to look straight at the place where the movement and the sound came from.

He had hoped to see nothing. But instead he saw The Animal.

What did it look like? He wasn't sure. It had legs and a tail, and two pale eyes that glowed in the half darkness. He stared at it, and it stared back at him. Then he heard it say, "Well? Am I like what you thought I'd be?"

Finn said, "I don't know. I didn't know what you'd be like."

"That's because you never looked at me properly," The Animal said.

"I can't see you very well."

"You aren't thinking very well. For instance, would you like me to be larger?" As it spoke, The Animal grew bigger in every direction, so that its head touched the ceiling of the room, and Finn could see legs reaching to each corner.

"No. I don't want you any bigger," Finn said in a hurry.

The room suddenly emptied of the shadowy shape. A very small voice near the floor said, "That better?"

Finn could just see the pinpoints of

light coming from two eyes near his feet. "I can hardly see you at all now. Only your eyes," he said.

"You're not easy to please," the very small voice said, but the eyes became larger, and there was a dark something between Finn and the window.

"But what are you really?" he asked.

"I'm whatever you think I am," said The Animal.

"So if I thought you were a tiger . . .?"

"I'd be a tiger." And suddenly, quite clear and distinct, there in front of Finn was a tiger. Full size, striped, with bristling whiskers and an alarming number of teeth. Finn said, "No! I don't want you to be a tiger!" Immediately the tiger vanished and the shadowy shape was there instead. Although he couldn't see it clearly, Finn had the feeling that it was laughing.

"Could you be . . . Could you be a rabbit?"

"Any time," said The Animal. Finn saw a rabbit, pale brown, with deliciously long

floppy ears, sitting on the seat of the basket chair, cleaning its whiskers. "See? I can be anything you think," it said.

"An elephant? Look out!" Finn cried, as he found himself squashed against the door by a huge grey bulk which was squeezing all the breath out of his body.

"A very small elephant," he managed to say, and found that the tickling sensation on the palm of his hand was being made by the stamping of an elephant the size of a fieldmouse. "Oh, lovely! Can't you stay like this?" he asked it.

"As long as you think of me like this," the tiny elephant said, running its minute trunk over the ball of Finn's thumb.

"How do you mean?"

"Don't you understand yet? I'm whatever you think I am. If you think I'm a tiger, then I'm a tiger. If you think I'm an elephant, then I'm an elephant. When you run upstairs in the dark, if you think I'm a bear, then I am a bear."

"A real bear? You mean, if you caught me, you'd eat me?"

"When I'm a bear. I do what bears do. I might just hug you tight."

"And when I'm in bed and it's all dark . . .?"

"I told you, I'm what you think I am. Last year, when you'd seen that wildlife programme on the telly, I was a hyena.

When I wasn't being a vulture."

"Hyenas pick people's bones," said Finn.

"That's right. That's what they do."

"Would you pick my bones?"

The Animal said: "If I was a hyena I might. Till you stopped me."

"How could I stop you?"

"I told you. By stopping thinking I was a hyena. I'm Your Animal."

"You mean, like my pet?"

The animal was now offended. Finn could tell, even in the dark, by the way its small feet pounded on his hand. "Certainly not! I am not a pet," said the tiny elephant's tiny voice.

"But you said you were mine. My Animal."

"I never said I was a pet. Pets are common, ordinary animals. Cats, dogs, mice, rabbits. They are REAL," said The Animal, in a voice which showed his scorn.

"Aren't you real?"

"Certainly not. I exist in your imagination.

14

You think me, therefore I am. Not like one of those boring creatures who always stay the same."

"If I had a dog, wouldn't he be my animal too?" Finn asked.

"Could he turn into something quite different if you wanted him to? A monkey? Or a crocodile, for instance?"

asked The Animal.

"No."

"Then wouldn't you rather have me?" said The Animal.

"Not when you're a tiger," Finn said.

"It's entirely your fault if I turn into a tiger. You just have to be careful how you think," said the tiny elephant.

"But when I'm frightened, I can't think quickly enough," Finn said.

"You'll have to learn."

"So if I was coming downstairs in the dark and I thought there was a bear behind me, I could quickly turn you into an elephant?"

"If I were you, I wouldn't choose to have an elephant coming down those stairs. Remember what your mum says when it's only you."

Finn considered this. It seemed to him that he was going to have to be careful how he thought, especially after dark.

"Has Locker got an animal too?"

"Of course. Everyone has an animal."

"Has my mum got an animal?"

The small elephant trumpeted scornfully. "She's like most grown-ups. It's not a proper animal, it's more like a human. But she certainly used to have one. It was generally a horse. I told you. Everyone has something."

"It's dark, and I'm in my bedroom and I'm not frightened," Finn said, surprised.

"That's because you've got me. You wouldn't be afraid to go downstairs with me now, would you?" the tiny elephant asked comfortably.

Finn walked down the stairs, without even listening for footsteps behind him. When he reached the last step, he stopped and looked at the little creature in his hand.

"What shall I do with you in the kitchen? I don't want Mum to know about you."

"She can't see me. No one can see anyone else's animal."

"How do I know you'll come back when I want you?" Finn asked, outside the kitchen door.

"You know, because I'm Your Animal. Unless you think about me, I haven't anywhere to be. I need you, Finn," said The Animal.

Finn's hand went out for the handle of the kitchen door. There was a small, soft scrabble against his palm. Then he was in the lighted kitchen, and his mum was saying, "That took you a long time. Anything wrong?"

Finn said, "No. Here're the trews, Mum," and handed them over.

"It took so long because he's frightened of the dark," said Locker, nastily.

"I'm not."

"You are."

Finn thought of the tiny elephant. Then he thought about the tiger and the bear and the hyena. "But really they are all My Animal," he thought. He remembered how he had made himself look at The Animal in his room. He said, "I'm frightened sometimes. But I'm not frightened all the time like I used to be."

And that was true too.

Finn-Trak

"What's the matter?" The Animal asked. It crouched, shadowy, at the end of Finn's bed, uncertain, until he had decided for it, what shape to take on.

"Locker was horrible to me," Finn said, rubbing his eyes.

"Why? And do make up your mind what I'm to be this evening," The Animal said, stretching enormously long limbs up to the ceiling, and then whisking around a tail like a mop.

Finn tried to think what sort of animal would be most comforting. "Could you be a rat? A white rat? A tame white rat?" he added, not fancying the idea of the sort of black creature who scuttles around rubbish bins.

The white rat sat up on top of the quilt covering Finn's chest, and delicately washed its face. It had a pink nose and

long, quivering whiskers, and it was as white as an advertisement for a washing powder. The rat and Finn looked at each other. Neither said anything.

"Tell me why Locker was horrible," the rat said at last. It curled its long tail round and sucked the end, just as Finn often sucked the end of his pen while he thought.

"He's lost his briefcase. It was new for his birthday and it's got a combination lock so it's very special, and it's got all his foreign stamps in it, so he's upset."

"Does he often lose things?"

"All the time. Last week he lost his purse with money in it. And yesterday he lost the front door key which was in his shirt pocket. Mum was furious. She says a burglar will find it and come and steal everything in the house."

"How long has Locker had his purse and those other things?"

"Ages. I don't know. Why?"

"Why don't we find them for him?" the rat inquired.

"How can we? We've all of us looked all over the house and the garden, and we didn't find anything. What's the use? It's dark now, anyhow. We wouldn't be able to see anything."

"Who said we'd have to be able to see?" the rat sneered.

"How do you find things if you can't see?"

"Oh, work it out for yourself! Just because you're only human, doesn't mean that animals are stupid too," the rat said.

"I know they're not. I read in a book that chimps and gorillas are as clever as people."

"Cleverer, I wouldn't wonder," the rat said.

"All right then, why don't you be a gorilla?" Finn said. He was getting tired of the rat's sharp answers. He felt the end of his bed sink under the weight of the enormous shape before his eyes made it out.

"Will you be able to sleep there?" he asked.

"I shall try. What about you?"

Finn didn't answer. His eyelids were already dropping. He couldn't stay awake any longer. He was just conscious of warmth seeping through the blankets at the foot of the bed.

In the morning, The Animal was gone. But its last remark went on puzzling Finn as he went through the school day. How did you look for lost things out of doors, at night? Why did it matter how long Locker had had his purse and his briefcase and everything?

He hadn't discovered any answers to these questions when he came home from school in the afternoon and found Locker not just still cross, but also very miserable, which was somehow worse. You can fight or be horrible back to an angry brother, but you cannot do either of these things when he is unhappy. Finn and his mum did their best, but Locker remained miserable. He did not want to play games, or watch television. The only thing he could bear, was to listen to their mother reading a detective story out loud to them; it was *The Hound of the Baskervilles*, and it was almost too exciting. Afterwards, Finn went up to bed looking behind him for enormous dogs with luminous muzzles, and even Locker insisted on having all the lights on in the passage and on the stairs.

"I'd like you to be a kitten tonight, please," Finn said to the shadow by the door. He felt soft fur under his chin, and a delicate cattish smell under his nose. He stroked the kitten's forehead. "You're nice like this," he said to it.

"Maybe. But not much use," the kitten said.

"Useful for what?" Finn asked.

"Useful for finding those things your brother has lost."

"I told you, it's no good looking at night."

"Oh do use your brains! If you have any. Which I sometimes doubt," the kitten said sharply, and at the same time, Finn felt its needly little claws against his cheek. He said, offended, "You needn't be so fierce. Why don't you explain?"

"Don't you remember that story your mum read you tonight? About the clever chap who solved mysteries? Shellfish Bones, wasn't he? Though shellfish really don't have bones. They have shells instead."

"Sherlock Holmes. What's that got to do with finding Locker's stuff?"

"Think! You can't be that stupid. How did the hound know to go after Sir Henry?"

"Oh! Oh! I see," Finn said, seeing slowly what His Animal meant and how really clever it was.

"If I wasn't a kitten. If I was . . ."

"If you were a bloodhound, you'd be able to smell . . ."

". . . track anything I knew the smell of . . ."

"Like Locker's purse and briefcase and . . . But do you know what Locker's briefcase smells like?" Finn asked.

"I presume it smells of Locker. That's why I asked you how long he'd had it."

"You'd better be a bloodhound . . ." Finn began, then stopped as the small, furry bundle on his chest suddenly swelled, became heavy and bony, and slid off the bed to stand beside it. In the dim light Finn saw the great head stretched over him, with the square muzzle above hanging folds of skin round the jaw. The bloodhound was impressively large.

"Now we can get down to business," the hound said. It had a deep, baying voice.

"Do you know what Locker smells like?" Finn asked.

"I shall refresh my memory," the hound said, padding towards the door.

"How?" asked Finn.

"I shall find Locker and have a sniff," the hound said.

"He's gone to bed."

"I suppose he doesn't smell different when he's in bed?"

"He won't like you going in and smelling him," Finn said.

"Oh very well! I don't have to help to find whatever it is he's lost," the hound said, offended.

"Do it tomorrow. It's Saturday, I don't have to go to school, and I'd like to see you find it. Mum'd be furious if I went out again tonight," Finn said.

"Suit yourself. Tomorrow, then," the hound said, clambering clumsily onto Finn's bed.

"You might leave room for me," Finn said.

The hound moved a couple of inches. "That better?"

"A bit. But just for tonight . . ."

"What?"

"Could you be that gorilla again?"

"Rats, kittens, hounds, now that gorilla. Do make up your mind!"

"Gorilla, please."

There was a sort of skirmish on the bed, then suddenly the bed springs squeaked and the weight lifted. The gorilla had leapt to the top of the wardrobe, just underneath the slope of the ceiling.

"I feel better higher up," it explained. It sneezed loudly. "Dust," it explained, then curled itself into a huge dark cushion. In the following silence, Finn fell asleep.

"Are you there?" Finn asked, sitting up in bed in the morning sun. Some light

30

shadows on the top of the wardrobe ran together like drops of quicksilver to make a shape that he could barely see. It had an outline, but no substance. He could see the wall through it.

"What are you now?" he asked.

"What do you want me to be?" the shadowy shape asked.

"Aren't you going to be a hound? So you can track Locker's briefcase?"

The shape slithered down to the floor, where Finn could just make out its vast head above his own on his pillow. He said, "Won't people be frightened if they see you like that?"

"They won't be able to see me. You'll just have to be careful you don't give me away. Come on, get dressed and let's go down. I can smell food."

Finn was nervous during breakfast. The hound was more interested than it should have been in everything that went on. Finn saw its head almost disappear inside the oven when his mother took out the sausages which were keeping warm there. He saw the hound's long red tongue skilfully remove the sausage nearest to it on the edge of the dish, and he felt uncomfortable when his mum exclaimed, "Seven sausages! It should be eight to the pound. I shall complain to the supermarket."

"They won't take any notice. You can't prove there weren't eight when you paid for them," Finn's dad said.

"But I didn't open the packet till this morning," his mum said.

"Did you count them then?"

"I didn't exactly count them, but I'd have noticed if there hadn't been eight."

"You can't have been noticing much. They're probably extra large."

"I don't think they are," Finn's mum said, puzzled.

"It's all right. I only want one," Finn said.

"Are you sure? Aren't you hungry? You feeling all right?"

"I'm all right," Finn said. He looked reproachfully at the hound, but the hound chose not to look back. Instead it slunk under the table.

Locker wriggled.

"What's the matter?" his mum asked.

"Something tickled my leg."

"It's the draught from under the door. I must try to get it fixed."

"Didn't feel like a draught. Felt more like . . . a dog."

"Don't be ridiculous, Locker. How could there be a dog in the kitchen?"

"A dog's nose. It was cold," Locker said.

"Just a nose without a dog, I suppose?"

Locker looked under the table. Finn froze. But Locker reappeared, shaking his head, puzzled. He hadn't seen the hound. But Finn could feel it, shifting its weight about round his legs. He took the piece of toast and marmalade from his plate and secretly held it below table level. He felt it taken gently from his hand by a large mouth.

"Finn, you're eating too quickly. You'll have indigestion if you swallow your toast like that," his mum said.

"Can I have another slice? I'll eat it as slow as you like," Finn said.

"I thought you weren't hungry."

"I wasn't hungry for sausages. I am for toast."

"Don't say sausages are going to be another thing you don't like. It'll be fish fingers next," Finn's exasperated mother said, tired of finding her sons taking a dislike to one kind of food after another.

"I'm still ravenous," the hound said after breakfast. It and Finn were alone in the passage leading to the front door.

"I'm sorry. But you shouldn't have eaten that sausage."

"I only ate one. I could have taken the lot."

"Do be careful! You could get me into a lot of trouble."

The hound did not answer this. It was streaking out of the door into the street.

"Where are you going?" Finn's mum said, seeing him disappearing out of the front door.

"Just going out. Won't be long." Finn couldn't wait. The hound had already set off, nose to the ground. "At any rate it's picked up Locker's smell," Finn thought, but he was disappointed when the hound stopped outside the next door but one. "Quite a strong clue here," the hound said as Finn caught up with it.

"But this is where Mrs Bellamy lives," Finn said.

"Perhaps she stole your brother's briefcase."

"She couldn't. She's about ninety. She hardly ever goes out."

"Then why is there a smell of Locker around her gate?"

Finn thought. Then he remembered. "She was in her front garden yesterday when we got back from school and we talked to her for a bit. We were standing here," he said.

"Very misleading. Let's go on," the hound said, starting off again.

It was a slow progress. The hound stopped at front gates, at doors, at lamp posts – though Finn wasn't quite sure whether that was really looking for Locker's briefcase or for a different purpose. Presently the hound went faster, with its nose to the pavement in a very purposeful manner. Finn had to run to keep up with it. It turned a corner, and he saw its tail disappearing through a gap in a fence. Finn reached the fence and looked through the gap. "Funny! That's Jamie's garden," he thought.

Nobody had cut the grass in Jamie's

garden for a very long time. All Finn could see of the hound was a tail just showing above the long stalks. The tail quivered, moved quickly to the left, and the hound's head appeared with something in its mouth. It lolloped over to the fence, pushed its way through the gap and laid something at Finn's feet.

"Great! It's Locker's purse! And the money's still there! How . . ."

"Easy. There's a really strong Locker smell. I got it even through the mouse scent. They'd been there last night, nasty interfering little things. And a cat or two. What else?"

"His briefcase? The front door key?"

It was an exhausting morning. The hound found traces of Locker's smell along all the roads near-by. It was amazing what a lot it discovered through its useful nose. "He stopped here for quite a time," he said, on the bank of the canal.

"Fishing," said Finn.

"Didn't catch anything, then. Not a

sniff of anything fishy. But he went across the road to that shop and bought himself an ice-cream. There's a sort of sweet, pinkish smell . . ."

"He's not supposed to buy ice-creams between meals," Finn said.

". . . and he sat down on that bench to eat it." The hound prowled round the bench. "Hi! What's this?"

Propped against the side of the iron bench, and half hidden by the litter bin standing next to it was a briefcase. Locker's. When Finn looked inside, he saw at once that the big envelope of foreign stamps was still there.

"You're fantastic!" Finn said.

"Any time. Just ask," the hound said, casually.

"Well . . . the front door key. I told you, Mum's worried that a burglar will find it."

The hound moved on, nose to ground. They passed the children's playground and the football pitch and came to the bridge over the railway line.

"He stopped here too. By the railing. This side and that side too. Wonder what he was doing?"

"Probably a train went past. But there isn't one due now for ages. Let's go on."

"Wait a tick. There's something shiny down there."

"An old tin can?"

"It's fastened to a bit of string, and the string's caught on a nail or something."

"Let me look," Finn said, leaning dangerously over the rail.

"Careful!" said the hound.

"It's a key! It's probably our key. It must have fallen out of his pocket. Let's get it."

"It's too far down for you to reach," said the hound.

"If you held on to my legs I might just be able to hook it off."

"I am certainly not going to do anything of the sort."

"But we can't just leave it there! Could you get it, d'you think?"

"Hounds don't climb," the hound said.

"They jump, though," Finn said, stupidly.

"Oh do try to use your addled little brains! What do you think I am?" the hound asked, exasperated.

"You're a hound. I mean . . . You're a dog."

"Try again. Stupid."

"You're . . ." Finn suddenly saw. "You're My Animal. So if I say you're . . . You're the gorilla," he shouted triumphantly, and almost before the word was out of his mouth, a large black animal had clambered down the struts at the side of the railway bridge and was reaching for the dirty piece of string.

* * * * *

"But where did you find it?" Finn's mum asked.

"It'd fallen off him when he was on the railway bridge."

"Over the edge? Finn, you didn't . . .? You know I've always told you not to climb down."

"I didn't. I . . . I managed to fish it up without climbing down at all." But 'fish', Finn thought was not the right word. He could have said, "I managed to gorilla it up."

"And you found the briefcase and his purse. Brilliant! Isn't he brilliant, Locker?"

"He's all right," Locker said, good tempered now he had his briefcase and his stamps again.

"How did you know where to look?" Finn's mum asked.

"Just looked everywhere Locker had been."

"I feel much better now we've got the house key back. Last night I was so anxious I kept on waking up, thinking I could hear burglars."

"I could make My Animal into a watch-dog. But would a burglar be frightened of a watch-dog he couldn't see properly?" Finn thought. Aloud he said, "Don't worry, Mum. If we did have a burglar I expect I could track him down too."

Toasted Cheese for Supper

Finn was putting on his pyjamas, when he had one of those disagreeable, cold thoughts about what might be underneath his bed. His Animal could be friendly, but it could also be frightening. Could it be a snake he wondered? Finn didn't fancy having a snake under his bed. But he remembered that when he'd had the courage to look straight at the Animal he had felt better about it and had got to know it. He bent down and peered.

There was something under the bed. It was a shadowy something with no particular shape, but with two holes in the darkness that might have been eyes. A shiver ran down Finn's spine. He said uncertainly, "Who are you?"

"You can't have forgotten already. I'm Your Animal," the Animal said.

"I hadn't exactly forgotten. I just wasn't

expecting . . . I thought you'd look like you did last night," Finn said.

"You have forgotten! I'm whatever you choose. And I wish you'd hurry up choosing, I don't enjoy being a sort of nothing like this."

"Sorry. Be a . . ." Finn thought quickly, and while he thought he climbed into bed. It felt safer than standing on the floor. "Couldn't you be that gorilla again?" He saw a huge furry outline begin to take shape. The size of the shape did not change. A black gorilla was weighing down the end of his bed.

"Right. What shall we do tonight?" the gorilla asked, scratching itself thoughtfully under one arm.

"Don't know. Tell me a story."

"Gorillas don't tell stories. It's not their scene."

"What would you have to be to tell stories?"

"An old man? Or an old woman?" For an instant the weight on the bed changed, and Finn saw a spidery old man in a tall

44

black hat, standing by his side. "Once upon a time there was a beautiful princess . . ."

"No, don't! I like you better the way you were!" Finn cried, and immediately the gorilla was there again, laughing.

"What do gorillas do?" he asked.

"Live in trees. Eat bananas. Thump their chests. Like this." The gorilla beat on its enormous chest and the room echoed with the sounds.

"Be careful! Mum might hear you!" Finn cried out.

"She can't hear me any more than she can see me. She'll hear you, though if you try it. But you wouldn't be able to make as much noise as me, your chest is too small."

"It isn't! I've got a very good chest."

"For a squitty little human, you may have, but it wouldn't be much catch if you were a gorilla," the gorilla said, pleased with itself.

Finn did not want to go on with this conversation so he said, "Well, what

45

shall we do?"

"Let's go out climbing," the gorilla suggested.

"Mum'd have a fit if she saw me going out now."

"She doesn't have to see you."

"Yes she does. She keeps the door of the living room open in the evening because the telephone's in the kitchen and so she can hear us if we have nightmares. She'd hear me going down the stairs," Finn said.

"We don't have to go down the stairs."

"I don't understand," Finn said.

"Window," the gorilla said briefly.

"How would we get down? Dad'll hear me if I try to get the ladder."

"Ladder! Who needs a ladder? There's a tree, isn't there?"

"Ye . . . es."

"Well then! It's easy."

"How do we get on to the tree?"

"Jump, stupid! I'll show you," the gorilla said.

Before Finn could say another word,

the gorilla was at the window and had wrenched it open. It crouched on the sill, then it flung itself out into the darkness. Finn heard the creak of the branches and he could just make out the top of the great tree against the night sky, bending and shaking with the gorilla's weight.

"Come on! What are you waiting for?" the gorilla called.

Before Finn could answer, he heard feet pounding up the stairs. He just had time to leap into his bed and pull the quilt up to his chin before his mum came into the room like a whirlwind.

"Finn?"

"Yes, Mum."

"You all right?"

"Yes, Mum. Why?"

"Didn't you hear it? That old tree outside your window. Dad and I heard it downstairs, cracking and groaning as if it were going to break. He went out into the garden to make sure it wasn't falling, and I came up here to see if . . ." What Finn's mum had really come for was to make sure that Finn hadn't somehow managed to get into the tree, but she didn't want to suggest that he might do such a thing, so she finished her sentence, ". . . to see if you'd heard it too."

"Yes, Mum. I did."

"A bit frightening, wasn't it?"

"Mmm. Is it going to break?" Finn asked.

"Why have you got your window open at the bottom? You know I don't like you going to sleep with it like that," Finn's mother said, going over to the window and shutting it.

"It's quite safe. I'm not going to jump out," Finn said, and meant it, whatever the gorilla did.

"Suppose you walked in your sleep?"

"Mum! I've never walked in my sleep."

"You don't know that you never will. Some people do, especially after they've eaten cheese for supper. You can leave the top bit open, that should give you enough air. Now go to sleep, Finn. I'm sorry if I woke you up, but I was a bit worried," his mum said, and she left, shutting the door behind her.

Finn waited until he heard her footsteps reach the bottom of the stairs, then he crept out of bed and opened the bottom of the window again. He was just about to call for His Animal, when he saw a figure at the foot of the tree. It seemed to be gazing up towards him.

"Hi!" he called softly.

"Finn? What are you doing out of bed at this time of the night?" his dad's voice answered.

"Just looking. I heard a funny noise . . ."

"I should think you did. Can't imagine what came over this old tree. Go back to bed, Finn. Time you were asleep hours ago. And SHUT THAT WINDOW," his dad suddenly bellowed. Finn shut the window. "But I'll have to open it again when Dad's gone in or how is My Animal going to get back?" he wondered.

He got into bed. He listened for the shutting of the door from the kitchen to the garden, which would tell him that Dad was safely inside the house again. He began to feel very sleepy. Several times he found that his head had fallen forward on to his chest and he jerked awake again with a start. He settled himself to wait in a more comfortable position and . . .

. . . to his astonishment, when he opened his eyes, the room was full of daylight, and his bedside clock told him that it was half past seven.

During the day, he wondered what had happened to the gorilla. It couldn't have climbed back through the small space at the top of the window that had been left open. He hoped it hadn't taken offence and left him for ever.

That evening, as he was getting ready for bed in the half dark, he said, experimentally, "You there?"

"Of course," said a voice from nowhere.

"Will you be that gorilla again?" Finn asked, and saw the gorilla, sitting on the chair in front of him.

"Any plans for the evening?" the gorilla asked.

"I don't understand. You said no one except me could see you, but Mum and Dad both heard you jump into that tree," Finn said. This had been puzzling him all day.

"They didn't hear *me*, stupid. They heard the tree. Like, if I ate one of their bananas, they wouldn't see me doing it, but they would miss the banana next day."

"How did you get back in last night? I

couldn't open the window again," Finn said, putting on his pyjama trousers.

"Didn't. I went for a rampage on the common. There's a thing there you climb up and slide down. Not bad," the gorilla said.

"You mean the slide in the playground? Yes, it's good fun."

"There's something much better a bit further on," the gorilla said.

"What's that?"

"There's a huge, enormous hole in the ground behind a fence . . ."

"I know. Where they're building the block of offices, and the new swimming baths."

"There's a great big crane there. I thought it would be fun to climb up it."

"You'd never be allowed!" Finn exclaimed.

"Who's to stop me? I told you, you're the only person who can see me. You could come too."

"They might not see you, but they'd see me," Finn said.

"All right. We'll go now, then, while it's darkish. Hurry up." The gorilla pushed up the bottom of the window.

"Mum'll kill me if she finds that window open again," Finn said.

"Come on, quickly then." The gorilla was poised on the sill, holding out a helping hand.

"I'm not going to jump on to that tree," Finn said, backing away.

"Quite safe. I'll help."

"Last night, Mum was upstairs a minute after you'd jumped, asking what the row was. She'll come up again if you go that way."

"Very well. No tree. But there's a drainpipe. I noticed it last night."

The gorilla disappeared. Finn leant out of the window and saw it sliding down the drain pipe, the top of which was a foot or two away from his window. The gorilla looked up and beckoned. Finn shook his head. "I can't reach the pipe from here," he whispered.

The gorilla came up to Finn's level

54

almost as easily as it had gone down. Its arm reached up and yanked Finn out of the window and on to the pipe, which creaked and shook under their combined weight. But it held. Ten seconds later Finn and the gorilla were standing on a flower-bed by the side of the house. The earth felt cool and crumbly under Finn's bare feet.

The gorilla led the way out of the garden and down the road. They passed the playground, its swings neatly tied to the posts for the night. Beyond it was the fence round the building site; it was a good solid fence, and it had spy holes through which you could observe the men at work inside.

"It's sure to be locked," Finn said, hopefully. He wasn't at all sure that he really wanted to go on to the building site, and he dreaded what the gorilla might do once it was there.

"Locks don't matter," the gorilla said, and as it spoke it hauled itself up to the top of the fence. "Come on!" it said, leaning down and clutching at Finn's left arm and shoulder.

Finn said "Ouch!" and found himself let down on the other side. He was on the building site.

There were several cranes of different sizes standing about. In the dim light from the street lamps outside, the top of the largest seemed to touch the sky.

"Come on!" the gorilla said, moving towards it.

"What are you going to do?"

"Not just me. You and me. We are going to climb up to the top of that thing and find out what it does and how it does it."

"I know what it does . . ." Finn began, but before he could finish the sentence, the gorilla had dragged him to the bottom of the crane, and had swung itself twenty feet up by the metal frame.

"Come on!" it said again.

Finn put a foot on the lowest crossbar and clutched at a sloping strut above him. But the distances between the bars were

too large and the metal hurt his hands. "I can't," he said.

"You poor feeble little humans!" the gorilla said, but it spoke quite kindly. It tucked Finn under a brawny gorilla arm and began again to climb. When it

released Finn, they were a hundred feet up in the air. Finn found himself balanced on an iron girder, with another going up into the sky behind him. He held on to it with both hands and looked down.

He wished he hadn't.

"Giddy? It won't last. I'm just going to see how everything works," the gorilla said, and Finn saw it walk confidently along the long horizontal arm. When it came back, it swung itself down to look in through the windows of the cab. He saw it reach in through the half-closed window. A light in the cab went on, then off, then on again. Then lights appeared at intervals along the full length and height of the huge crane. "I do wish it wouldn't do that. Someone's sure to see," Finn thought.

"Good view you get from here. What's that building over there?" the gorilla asked.

"I don't know."

"You aren't looking."

"I don't want to look. I want to get down."

"I thought you'd enjoy being a long way up on a crane."

"I might like it inside the cab, not out here," Finn said, miserably.

"Get inside then," the gorilla said, opening the door of the cab and pushing Finn in.

It felt safer inside than out. In front of the driver's seat there were several interesting looking levers, and on the floor of the cab there were two foot pedals. While Finn was wondering what each one did and thinking he'd like to try them out, the gorilla had seated himself and had pulled two or three levers. Finn saw the long arm of the crane swing round, and from its end the metal hook on its hoist ropes dropped quickly down towards the ground.

"Great! Look what I'm doing!" the gorilla said.

"I wish you wouldn't. Someone might see," Finn said.

"Let them. They can't do anything about it."

"It's all right for you. No one can see you. But I'll be in terrible trouble if any one catches me here."

"Don't fuss. I'll get you down before anyone can say 'King Kong!' Now watch. I'm going to pick up that little hut over there, see if I don't."

The gorilla pulled lever after lever. Finn saw the huge hook go down closer to the hut, but still not near enough to touch it. Sometimes it swung to one side, sometimes to the other. But at last it was hovering just above the roof of the hut, where, after scrabbling about for some time, it managed to engage itself with something. Finn couldn't see what. Then the gorilla pulled another lever, and the hook rose into the air, carrying with it a large piece of the hut's roof.

"Told you I'd do it!" the gorilla said, triumphant. But Finn, looking down, was horrified. He could now see right into the hut, where a man stood, staring up into the sky. The man ran out of the hut door and began waving his arms and shouting. Finn could just hear the angry noise, a hundred feet below.

"Now you've done it! That must be the night watchman, and you've taken off the top of his hut," he said.

"He must be surprised," the gorilla said, pleased with itself.

"Get me down! You said you'd get me down. I don't want anyone to find me here," Finn said. He was sure that operating a crane when you weren't supposed even to be on the building site, was some sort of crime. He didn't want to be put in prison for something that a stupid gorilla had done.

"Don't you want a turn? Now I know which of these handles is which I could teach you quite easily."

"No! I just want to be on the ground!"

"Oh, all *right*, but you don't know what you're missing," the gorilla said. It scooped Finn up, held him tightly against a hairy chest and, scorning the ladder, scuttled down the crane's outside framework faster than any lift. The crisscross of the metal struts flew past Finn's eyes like a flying pattern of diamonds and crosses. The gorilla put him down on the safe ground with a thump that told him how annoyed it was. "I can't think why you didn't enjoy that more. I find it exhilarating to be up high like that," it said.

"Ex . . . what?"

"Exhilarating. Exciting. Makes life seem really worth living."

Finn had opened his mouth to reply to this, when there was a sudden sound of voices and a glare of light. The whole of the building site was illuminated by the overhead arc-lights. There was a crowd of people, too, spreading over the broken ground. Some of them were coming towards him. Finn thought, "Oh no! How am I going to explain a gorilla?"

He need not have worried about that.

By the time the first group reached him, Finn was alone.

"You been up in that crane?" someone asked him.

"What you doing here, anyway? Children aren't allowed on building

sites," someone else said.

"Who left the power on? Power shouldn't be left on," a third voice said.

"How'd you get in? Door was locked," the second voice said.

"Who took the roof off my hut? Someone took the top off my hut," another voice broke in. Finn saw the night watchman, again. He had looked tiny from the top of the crane, but close too, he was large and red and angry.

"Vandals!"

"Bovverboys!"

"No discipline nowadays! Disgraceful!"

Remarks like these flew around Finn's head. Someone was saying doubtfully, "He doesn't look old enough to work a crane," when an exclamation made everyone look up. The big arm of the crane was swinging round again, and the hook was coming down. It swung for a moment over the head of the night watchman, then it hooked itself into the belt of his overalls, picked him up and carried him across to the outside fence

65

and over it. When it rose again the struggling figure had been left behind and sounds of fury from beyond the fence could plainly be heard. Finn imagined that he could hear, too, the sound of laughter coming from a long way above them.

So after all he did not have to defend himself against the charge of working the crane. Everyone had seen that whoever had picked up the night watchman could not have been Finn, who was standing next to them in his pyjamas. But it was difficult to explain how he came to be there at all.

"But I don't understand. Why did you go to the building site? And with bare feet!" his mum said.

"I don't know," Finn said.

"What did you think you were going to do there?" his dad asked.

"I don't know. I don't think I really

meant to go there," Finn said.

"How did you get out of the house without us hearing you?"

"They said someone was working the big crane. Lifted the night watchman's hut right off the ground, with him inside. Terribly dangerous. Did you see that?"

Finn nearly said, "It was only the roof, and he wasn't inside it." Then he realised he had better say nothing.

"One woman said she thought she'd seen someone climbing up the side of the crane. That wasn't you, was it, Finn?"

"I expect he was walking in his sleep," Locker said.

"Sleep walking! I always said he might. Did you, Finn?"

"Not exactly," Finn said. He really couldn't begin to explain about the gorilla.

"You see? That's why you really must keep your window shut at night. And no more toasted cheese for supper," Finn's mum said. That was a pity, because Finn loved toasted cheese.

Finn's Mistake

It was a week before Christmas, and Finn's friends were talking about what they expected to get as presents.

"My dad's going to give me a bicycle," James said.

"My dad's giving me a radio–controlled aeroplane," Nicky said.

"I'm going to get two rabbits, and they're going to have lots and lots of babies," Melanie said.

"Rabbits are stupid. You can't train rabbits to do tricks," Joey said.

"Our dog can go to the shop and bring back the newspaper," Sally said.

"My uncle's got a sheepdog who won in a trial on the telly," said Colin.

Finn had opened his mouth to say that there was a bird in their street which had discovered how to tweak off the foil tops of milk bottles to get at the cream. But now he shut his mouth again. A dog who had won a sheepdog trial was far more exciting than a stealing bird.

"I know someone who keeps a monkey," Joey said.

"I know someone who's got a tame fox," someone else said.

"A real, live fox?"

"It lives in a shed at the back, and they give it scraps."

"What are you getting for Christmas?" Nicky asked Finn.

Finn didn't know. His mum had talked about getting him a camera, or a watch. But cameras and watches seemed dull compared to bicycles and monkeys and foxes. He thought of His Animal, which could take any shape he chose, and he said, "I'm going to get a boa constrictor."

No one seemed much interested.

"What's a boa constrictor?" Sally asked.

"A snake. A big huge snake that winds itself round animals and squashes them to death," Finn said.

"Yuk! I wouldn't want a snake like

that," Melanie said.

"Where could you keep it?" Nicky asked.

"I don't know. Somewhere."

"Won't your mum mind?" James asked.

"Not as long as I train it so it isn't a nuisance," Finn said.

"Who's going to give you it?" Joey asked.

"My uncle who lives abroad," Finn said.

"I don't believe you. You're making it up," Joey said.

"I'll bring it to school next term. Then you'll see," Finn said. By next term, he reckoned, Joey would have forgotten about the boa constrictor.

Finn forgot about it too. For the next two days he didn't think about anything except Christmas. Helping Mum to make the pudding – "Should have made it months ago, but I expect it'll be all right," she said. Wrapping up his presents for other people, hanging up paper chains and tinsel round the living room, trying to make the fairy lights on the Christmas tree stay lit up. (They wouldn't.) At last, it was time to hang up his stocking before he went to bed. It wasn't really his stocking, it was one of Dad's huge thick walking stockings that came right up to the knee, so that it could hold a lot more than one of Finn's own. Locker had the other one to hang up at the end of his bed. At last it was quite late on the night before Christmas. Finn was alone in his bedroom and all he had to do was to shut his eyes and go to sleep and then, very soon, it would be Christmas Day.

He went to sleep quite quickly. He dreamed that he was Father Christmas, going the rounds with presents for kids, but nothing went quite right. First of all, the reindeer kept stopping and saying they needed their tanks filled, and Finn didn't know how to satisfy them. Then he worried that he hadn't got enough presents for all the children he should be visiting, and finally, when he had succeeded in persuading the reindeer to land him on a roof, he couldn't get down the chimney, but stuck, with his head and shoulders outside and the rest of him wedged in a chimney. It began to snow. His shoulders were freezing.

He woke up with a start. His duvet had somehow managed to wind itself tightly round his legs and behind and his top half was uncovered and very cold. He turned on his bedside light so that he could re-arrange himself comfortably.

His bedroom looked quite different. The stocking he had hung up was no longer flat and empty. It was bulging and something, he couldn't quite see what, stuck out of its top end. And there were parcels stacked underneath it. A long thin parcel and a knobbly, interesting looking parcel done up with brown paper, a square box-shaped parcel and several small packets with bright paper and ribbons.

It was a rule in Finn's house that you didn't open your Christmas presents until the morning. Open them properly, that is. But if you happened to have torn a corner of the paper, or loosened the string before it was quite daylight, no one was going to take much notice. Finn got out of bed to investigate. First, he shook some of the smaller packets. One of them rattled, but it didn't sound like money, more like marbles. Another smelled deliciously of chocolate. Finn's mouth watered. Two very neatly packed parcels were certainly books. He turned his attention to the large knobbly parcel; he pushed it a little and found that it was softer in some places, harder in others. It was a most peculiar shape. The brown paper was loose, and Finn managed to prize open a fold so that he could see inside. It was red, his favourite colour, looked like some sort of sack . . . then he realised. It was a backpack, exactly what he'd been wanting. He tidied up the paper so that the place he had peeped through didn't show.

He opened the chocolate smelling packet and took a bite from a Mars bar.

He felt happy. There were still plenty more parcels to open and he enjoyed trying to guess what might be in them.

It was clear that he wasn't going to get all the things he'd asked for. He had suggested a puppy, but both Mum and Dad had told him straight out that he should give up that idea at once. "If we lived in the country . . ." Mum had said, and Dad had said, "No way am I going to have a dog in this house." A bicycle? Not likely; he'd have to put up with Locker's old machine when Locker had grown out of it, just as he'd had to put up with Locker's old tricycle and sometimes, when they were not too ragged, Locker's second-hand clothes. A radio-controlled aeroplane, like Nicky's? Almost certainly not; he knew that those radio-controlled toys were very expensive. He remembered Melanie and her rabbits; Finn definitely didn't want rabbits for Christmas. Nor did he really want a fox, though he would quite have liked a real gorilla.

It was at this moment that he

remembered what he had told his friends about his Christmas present. He had said he was going to get a boa constrictor. It had been all very well to say that in the daylight, surrounded by friends, but now, in the night, when he was alone, he should try not to think about a boa constrictor, or any other kind of snake.

But once a thought has come into your head, it is extremely difficult to un-think it. Finn tried. He tried so hard that he stopped eating the Mars bar. But it was no good. He was still thinking, "One of my presents is a boa constrictor."

The large brown paper parcel moved. Finn had propped it up against the bookcase. It now fell over. Finn sat and stared at it. He said to himself, "It just fell over." But he couldn't be sure. And then, just as he had made up his mind that it had been the sort of accident that happens when you haven't propped something up securely, the parcel moved again, this time along the floor towards him.

"No!" Finn cried out, terrified.

The parcel moved a little nearer.

"No! I don't want . . ." Finn began, and then he heard the sound of a door opening and feet coming towards his room. His cry must have woken Mum. In a split second, Finn was back in bed. He had turned off the light, just before his own door was opened and Dad's voice said, "Finn? Anything the matter?"

Finn wished he could snore. He

couldn't, so instead, he said, in a sleepy voice, as if he'd just woken up, "Who's that?"

"It's me, Dad. You were calling out, didn't you know?"

"I sort of heard something," Finn said, not wanting to lie too much.

"Must have been dreaming. Go back to sleep, Finn. It isn't time to wake up for Christmas yet." Dad left. As soon as Finn had heard him shut his own door, he turned on his torch and looked at the parcel.

"Are you My Animal?" he asked. He was shaking, but then he'd been out of bed and it was cold.

"Get me out of here," a voice said, muffled by nylon and brown paper. The parcel shook furiously.

"I'll try," Finn said. It was not a task he fancied. Nor was it easy. Although the brown paper had been loosely wrapped round the backpack, it was fastened with far too much sticky tape. That was Dad's doing, he always did up his parcels with this horrible tape which was impossible to peel off, and difficult to cut. What made the job worse was that inside the parcel there was something large and moving, and impatient. Finn was frightened. It might be His Animal, but he'd never seen it as a snake before, and he was sure it was going to be furious with him when at last he got it out.

That did not happen until he had fetched the penknife from his desk and cut enough of the tape and the paper to free the zip at the top of the backpack. As soon as he'd pulled the zipper back, a head shot out followed by what seemed yards of brown and yellow body, which slithered across the floor and then arranged itself in coils. The head fixed Finn with a beady black eye.

"Don't ever do that to me again," the boa constrictor said.

"Do what?" Finn asked.

"Think of me inside something that I can't get out of. I might have suffocated."

"Sorry! I didn't mean to. It was because

I was talking to Nicky about Christmas presents."

"Excuse me. It isn't what you talk about to your friends that decides what I am and where. It's how you think of me when you're alone. You thought of me trapped inside that . . . that thing!" the boa constrictor said.

"That's because I was thinking about how you might be a Christmas present."

"Why should that mean having all that paper and stuff round me?"

"Because people always do wrap up Christmas presents. Like that," Finn said, pointing to the other parcels and packets lying around.

"I wouldn't have been able to get into any of those. Too small. What's inside them?" the boa constrictor asked.

"I'm not sure. Those two must be books. That one had some chocolate." Finn remembered the Mars bar. It was lying half out of its packet. He picked it up and showed it to the boa constrictor.

"You've eaten half of it!" the boa

constrictor said.

"Do you want a taste?" Finn held the remains of the bar out towards the boa constrictor's mouth, but the boa constrictor drew back, with an expression of disgust.

"No thank you. Not quite what I am used to. I suppose you haven't got any proper food here?"

"What's proper food?" Finn asked.

"A rat? A mouse, even? I suppose it's too much to ask for a young rabbit?"

"I haven't got anything like that."

"I shall investigate," the boa constrictor said. Finn watched its long mottled body wreathing itself round the packets, sniffing at each one, and leaving it, disappointed. "I wonder if My Animal can be more than one thing at a time? If it could, I could think of it as a rat and then the boa constrictor could eat it. Only it'd be eating itself," Finn thought. It was a muddled thought. He was getting very sleepy.

"Wake up!" the boa constrictor said

sharply.

"I'm not asleep."

"You're not far off it. What do you want to do?"

"I'd really like to go back to bed and go to sleep again."

"That's not very adventurous. Think of something more interesting."

"It's the middle of the night," Finn objected.

"We've done things in the middle of the night before now."

"But it's Christmas tomorrow. If I don't go to sleep now, I won't be able to stay awake for it."

If a boa constrictor could shrug its shoulders, this boa constrictor did. Finn felt that it despised him for being so feeble. It said, "Oh, very well. Go back to bed, if that's what you want."

Finn got back into bed. The boa constrictor lay on the floor and looked at him. Somehow Finn didn't much like the way it was looking.

"So what am I supposed to do now?" it

asked.

"Couldn't you go to sleep too? After all, it is night."

"I am a nocturnal animal," the boa constrictor said.

"What does that mean?"

"Means I'm awake all night. I sometimes sleep during the day."

"Well, I'm not a noc . . . what you said. I want to go to sleep now," Finn said.

The boa constrictor moved quickly. Finn saw its head appear over the side of the bed and felt its weight coiling across the duvet. "Is it warm in there? I'm cold," it said, wreathing itself round on Finn's chest.

"No!" Finn said, pulling the duvet as tight as he could round his neck to prevent the boa constrictor from getting under it.

"That's not fair! I let you go to sleep, when I really want to do something exciting, and now you won't even let me in under this cover so that I can warm up. Don't you know that snakes are cold blooded animals?" the boa constrictor asked.

"I thought that meant you didn't feel the cold."

"It means that I find places where I can get warm. The country I come from is hot. This place is cold. I shall freeze if I have to stay out here all night."

Finn couldn't bear the thought of having a boa constrictor under his duvet. But however much he tried, he couldn't think hard or clearly enough to turn His Animal into anything but the boa constrictor it was. He was so sleepy and it was so very large and heavy, so very brown and yellow, so very near. He said, "Look! I'll find something to keep you warm, I promise. Only not my duvet. I wouldn't be able to sleep at all if you were under here with me."

"Where, then?" the boa constrictor asked.

Finn shone his torch round his room. There was coloured paper, the end of a Mars bar, the half unwrapped backpack on the floor. He saw his clothes on the chair. "You could wrap yourself in my pullover?" he suggested.

The boa constrictor slid off the bed and investigated the chair. If Finn hadn't been so sleepy and frightened he'd have laughed to see the creature trying to get into his pullover. It got its head into a sleeve and stuck there. When it had jerked itself free, it put its head out of the neck opening and its tail appeared at the end of the other sleeve. But it was clear that the pullover wasn't nearly big

enough. It wouldn't cover even half of the great snake's body.

"What's that?" it asked suddenly, pointing with its nose.

"That's my Christmas stocking."

"What's it got in it? Anything for me to eat?" But before Finn could answer that question, the boa constrictor had slithered across and caught the stocking in its mouth and had pulled it down to the floor. Finn saw it rapidly tip out the contents on to the floor. Finally, after a good deal of writhing and what sounded like cursing, it managed to cover itself almost completely underneath Finn's pullover and the stocking.

"That's better," Finn heard it say.

"But you've spilled all my stocking presents! and you've bitten a hole in Dad's stocking toe!"

"Of course if you'd rather I came into bed with you . . .?" the boa constrictor said, sticking its head out from under the woolly mountain.

"No!"

"Very well, then. Now, keep quiet."

"I'm going to sleep now," Finn said. He hoped the boa constrictor would stay where it was. He didn't fancy it back on his bed, trying to find a way to get under the duvet.

He switched off the torch. Nothing moved in the darkness. Finn slept.

★ ★ ★ ★ ★

"Wake up!"

"Wake up!" It was Locker's voice.

"Wha . . . at? What's the matter?" said Finn, still asleep.

"It's Christmas! It's morning. Well, almost." Locker turned on the light.

"What happened? You've taken everything out of your stocking! You've made a horrible mess," he said, and Finn had to agree. On the floor by his bed lay his pullover, his Christmas stocking, and various small objects which it had contained, as well as torn paper, a tangerine, shreds of ribbon and coloured paper. The boa constrictor had not been idle during the night.

"Mum won't be pleased," Locker said.

"I didn't mean . . ." Finn began.

"You'd better clear up that mess before she comes in. I'll help," Locker said, full of Christmas kindness. Finn saw him put out a hand towards the stocking. "Take care!" he'd cried out before he knew he was going to say anything.

"Take care of what? It's not going to bite," Locker said.

Finn thought of saying, "No, but it might wind itself round you and crush you to death." But as he looked, Locker picked up the stocking, which hung, flat and empty from his hand.

"You're still dreaming," Locker said, busily putting the stocking-fillers back where they belonged.

"I'm all right. Thanks, Locker. Have you opened your stocking yet?"

"Brought it in here so we can open them together, like always. I ate my Mars bar. Did you?"

"I ate some of it." Finn looked around. "It doesn't seem to be here," he said.

"I expect you ate the rest of it in your dream. Here's your stocking. Now, let's open them at the same time. One, two, three, Go!"

But though Finn later searched very carefully all over his now tidy bedroom floor, he never found the second half of the Mars bar. It seemed that the boa constrictor must have been starving as well as cold. "So it was real enough to eat. I wonder if anyone else would be able to see the Mars bar when they couldn't see the boa constrictor outside it?" Finn wondered. It was a puzzling thought.

Crocodiles in the Plumbing

Finn was pleased when it was Spring again. No more evenings when he had to go up to bed in the dark. Quite often he managed to go to sleep before the sky outside had lost all its light. This meant that he wasn't seeing much of His Animal, but it was comforting to know that it was there if he needed it.

One evening, when they'd finished washing the supper dishes, and Locker was watching the water swirl away down the plug hole of the sink, he said, "Did you know that in America they have crocodiles in their water pipes?"

"Who said?" Finn asked.

"I read it in the papers."

"How'd they get into the water pipes? Anyway, I don't believe it. They're too big," Finn said.

"They get there when they're babies.

People get them for pets, when they're tiny, and then when they are bigger, they're tipped down the loo, and they go on living in the drains. In the sewers."

"Are sewers big enough for them when they grow up?"

"Plenty big enough. Men can walk about in them. But the crocs don't stay down in the sewers, they start coming out of those gratings you get in the roads. Or up out of the lavatory. And they're hungry, because there isn't much to eat in a water pipe," Locker said, pleased at the idea.

But Finn was not pleased. When he was in the bathroom that night, he shut the lid of the lavatory carefully, and he looked at it several times, as he lay in the bath. Once he almost thought he saw the lid begin to rise, as if something, some enormous snout, was pushing it up from inside. He got out of the bath very quickly and put the weighing machine on top of the lid. "You won't be able to push that up," he said out loud. As he got into bed, he was grateful that there wasn't a fitted basin in his bedroom.

But as soon as he was in bed, he began to think about crocodiles again. He could just imagine a very small crocodile squirming its way along a water pipe, gasping for air, making for the nearest plug hole. In his mind, the crocodile grew very fast. At first it had only been a few inches long, but the more he thought about it, the larger it became, and now it was full size and lying alongside his bed, waiting for him to put a foot out, when . . . SNAP! He would have lost a foot, possibly a whole leg.

Something on the floor grunted and sighed. He heard a creak and a scaly sort of noise. He opened his mouth to scream, then found that he couldn't. He was too frightened.

He didn't know how long he had been lying there, stiff with fear. After what seemed like hours, he heard Locker coming upstairs and going into his own room. The door hinges squealed. They always did. Finn would have liked to call out for company, but he didn't want Locker to know that he was frightened. He lay still. He heard Locker taking off his shoes. Thump. Then, after a pause, another thump. He heard Locker walking around in his room with bare feet, pad, pad, pad. Then he heard the creak of the bed as Locker got into it. At the same time he heard the scaly, rustling noise from the floor by his own bed. His heart jumped. The crocodile really was down there.

He could just imagine Locker saying, "Don't be stupid! How could there possibly be a crocodile in your room? You're a baby!"

And he couldn't go downstairs to find his mum and pretend that he wanted a drink of water, or that he had a pain, because he couldn't put his foot out of bed in case the crocodile got hold of it.

And then he remembered His Animal. He sat up in bed and said, in a voice that didn't tremble much, "Hi!"

"Hi yourself," said a deep voice.

Somehow, when Finn heard that voice, he knew that it came out of an enormous big mouth with a great many teeth.

"You're a crocodile?" Finn said.

"Of course I'm a crocodile. That's what you were thinking, wasn't it?"

"But you're My Animal?"

"Of course I'm Your Animal! How many times do I have to explain? It's because I'm Your Animal that I have to be whatever you think I am. Tonight you wouldn't think about anything except crocodiles. So here I am. Your choice. Not mine."

"So if I think about you being something different, you'll be that?"

"Indubitably."

"What's that mean?" Finn asked, confused.

"It means, 'Yes, no question.' You think of something different, and that's what I'll be," the deep voice answered.

Finn lay back on his pillow and tried to think of a different animal. Something he wouldn't be frightened of. Something

94

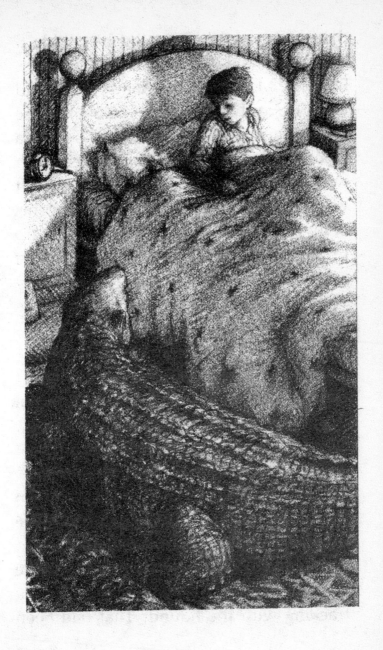

that might even be fun. But he couldn't. Even if he said to himself, "Dog. Cat. Squirrel. Mouse. Woolly lamb," his mind wasn't really thinking about these creatures. All the time he was seeing a crocodile, huge and scaly and green, with wicked little eyes and snapping jaws. It was slithering about on the rug by his bed. Now it was reaching its snout up towards him. He let out a very small part of a yell.

"What's the matter?" the crocodile asked.

"I just thought . . ."

"You aren't thinking at all. You haven't thought of one different kind of animal properly. You keep thinking 'Crocodile'. So I'm still here."

"Sorry," Finn said, ridiculously.

"Don't mind me. It's much the same to me what I am. Only we don't seem to be having much fun like this do we?"

Perhaps it was the word 'fun' that made Finn feel different. It reminded him of tracking with the hound. That had been fun. So, in a way, though it had been scary, was the adventure on the building site with the gorilla. He agreed with what the crocodile had said. It wasn't fun to lie here, in a cold sweat of terror because he'd imagined a crocodile on the mat by his bed. It was especially stupid when he could choose to turn the crocodile into something more interesting.

"Do you have to be a real animal?" he asked.

"Real, how? Like that tortoise who's supposed to live in your garden, but who never turns up when he's wanted?"

"No. I meant, real like animals you see in zoos. Like crocodiles. I mean, could you be an invented animal?"

"What sort of invented animal?" the crocodile asked.

Finn thought of stories he'd heard. Fairy stories, myths, legends. Giants, dwarfs, mermaids, dragons. He didn't want a scary monster, he wanted . . . And then he knew. "Could you be a horse with wings? I've read about one, called . . ." But before he could begin to say the name, he saw Pegasus standing by the bed.

"Oh! You're . . ." He wanted to say, "You're beautiful!" but that wasn't the sort of thing he was used to saying, so he didn't finish the sentence. But Pegasus was beautiful. He was a very pale golden brown, with a long, satiny nose and sad, wise eyes. His mane was paler than his coat, it shone like silver, and from his strong but slender back, soared two huge

wings, the feathers gleaming.

"That's better," Pegasus said. He put down his nose into Finn's hand and nuzzled it gently. "Now. Let's go!" he said.

"Where to?" Finn asked.

"Wherever we like. But you'll have to open the window. Hooves aren't any good for that."

Finn opened the bottom of his window very carefully. He did not want Mum rushing upstairs to find out what he was up to. He was lucky. The bottom of the sash window slid upwards with hardly a sound. "On my back!" Pegasus ordered, and Finn found himself sitting between the wings and clutching the silver mane, as the great horse leapt towards the window and was somehow through it, and climbing, climbing away from the ground and up towards the stars.

"You all right?" Pegasus asked, turning his head towards Finn.

"I'm all right," Finn said. It sounded so feeble that he allowed himself to say, "It's great, riding on your back."

Pegasus flew on. Finn saw the lights of a town far below them, with a lighted road curling among the pale fields and darker woods of open country. Then more street lights and the bright squares of house windows. Finn had been in an aeroplane, but he'd never flown low enough to be able to pick out what was happening on the earth below.

"Where are we going?" he asked again, but Pegasus did not answer, he just flew steadily on. "He must know where he's taking me," Finn thought, and wondered where he'd find himself when they came down to earth again. The rush of wind against his face and the ripple of the horse's muscles against his legs, was regular and monotonous. He shut his eyes against the wind and his head sank on his chest. Flying out over the world, on a mythical beast, Finn slept.

When he woke, he was sure he must still be dreaming. He should have been in his bed at home, opening his eyes on the

familiar things in his room. Books, his old toy penguin, posters on the walls, his clothes in a heap on the chair. But what he saw was quite different. He was lying on a sandy, pebbly shore, looking out over the sea. Near to his feet, small waves were breaking with little splashing sounds and then pulling back with the whisper of water draining through the stones. The sky over the horizon was just beginning to lighten and redden. The murmuring sea was a strange purple colour. Above him he could see a few fading stars.

He looked around for Pegasus. The horse was standing at the edge of the sea. A very small wind caught his mane and blew it sideways, and just ruffled the great wings. Otherwise he might have been a statue.

"Pegasus!" Finn called, and the horse turned and came up the strand towards him.

"Where are we?"

The horse said, "You would call it a

Greek island." Then he said, "When I lived on earth, this was my country. I wanted to see it again. I might never have another chance."

"Why not? Can't you fly here whenever you want?"

"Can I fly here when I'm a crocodile? Or a gorilla? Or a dog?"

"But . . . You don't have to be crocodiles and dogs. You can always be Pegasus," Finn said.

"You're forgetting. I'm Your Animal. I have to be what you think I am," the Animal said.

"What are you really?" Finn asked.

"I keep on telling you. I'm Your Animal. I'm whatever you choose for me to be. Once I was a hound, another time I was a snake. Today I'm a winged horse."

"No, but inside. Who are you? What do you feel like? You can't be all the things I think about and not have any inside for yourself."

"I feel like whatever you've turned me into. Of course if you decided that you

103

didn't need me any longer, then I could stay in one shape. I could be one creature. For ever."

"Wouldn't that be boring?"

"I don't know. I've never tried it."

"But you'd like to go on being Pegasus now?"

The horse bowed his head. His silver mane flowed in the slight sea wind. He pawed the ground with a delicate hoof. "If you didn't need me."

Finn remembered the first time he had seen His Animal. It was the first time he had felt brave enough to look properly at whatever might be there. Since then, he had not been so frightened in the dark. He said, "You mean, I needed you because I was frightened?"

"Everyone is frightened sometimes. It would be stupid not to know what fear is. If you had no imagination, you wouldn't be frightened, but you would be a simpleton. Your fear is your strength."

"I'm not as frightened as I used to be," Finn said.

"Because you learned how to turn me into a friend instead of an enemy."

"But if you stayed here, I wouldn't have you as a friend. If I got frightened, I wouldn't be able to turn the bear or whatever it was into you."

"No."

"What would you be doing?" Finn asked.

"That would depend on you."

"How? Why would it depend on me?"

"It would depend on how you thought me before you told me to go."

"So if I thought of you like this, you'd stay being Pegasus?"

"Yes."

"But if I thought of you being a slug, you'd stay being a slug?"

"That's right."

"If I said I'd be able to manage without you, could I ever see you again? Could I call you back?" Finn asked.

"Not in the way you can now. You wouldn't see me. We wouldn't be able to have adventures together."

"But I could remember you?"

"You could remember me."

"Couldn't I have something of yours to keep, so that you wouldn't seem so far away?" Finn asked.

"Take a hair from my mane. That way you won't forget," Pegasus said.

Finn looked at the silver mane. "I haven't got a knife. It'll hurt you if I just pull it out," he said.

"Don't worry about that. Pull."

Finn separated the long thick hairs, found one and pulled. He felt the winged horse quiver.

"Wind it round your finger for now. When you are at home, you can plait it into a ring."

"Will it be there when I'm at home?" Finn asked.

"As long as you need it," the horse said.

"So it's up to me now, what happens?"

"It is for you to decide," Pegasus said. He laid his golden head on Finn's shoulder and together they looked out over the dancing waves.

"The water's a funny colour. Not like English sea," Finn said.

"The wine-dark sea. That's what the Greek poets called it," Pegasus said.

The little waves curled near their feet. Finn was amazed at his own thoughts. He had power over this splendid creature by

his side. He could turn him into anything he liked – a wild beast, a trained dog, an insect. But he didn't want to turn him into anything else. He wanted him to stay as he was. Then he thought about being without His Animal, who had protected him through the nights and had taught him how to manage his own fear. He was still a little frightened. He wanted to keep His Animal. But more than anything, he wanted the winged horse to be free.

"I shall miss you," Finn said.

"You are strong. You can brighten the dark with your imaginings," Pegasus said.

"But if I let you go now, how am I going to get home?" Finn cried.

"I will take you back to your bed, and when you wake in the morning, you will think of this as a dream."

"It isn't a dream, is it? I don't want it to be a dream," Finn said, anxious.

"Climb on my back, and sleep, as you did while we came here. And tomorrow, think of me here, on my island, and remember that you have given me my freedom."

Finn climbed on to Pegasus' back and stroked the silver mane.

"Now, look once more at the sea and the mountains, and then shut your eyes and sleep," Pegasus said. Finn looked. It was still not really daylight, and he couldn't see much, but he could smell the salt on the wind and he could hear the little waves coming up the beach and drawing back, up and back, up and back. He felt the lift of the strong body beneath him and heard the regular beat of those huge wings. He bent forward so that his

face was pressed against the silky mane, and slept.

He woke. It wasn't morning, which was what he had expected. It was still dark. But he knew from the feel of the duvet under his chin and from the ticking of his bedside clock, that he was back in his own bed again. He looked round the nearly black room. He had a moment's panic when he remembered the crocodile which had been waiting for him on the mat by the bed. But then he remembered that this was the place where he had seen Pegasus, the winged horse. Then he thought of the island where Pegasus had taken him. He remembered the murmuring sea, the small salt wind, the black mountains and that golden shape standing by the sea's edge and sniffing the free air. Had he been dreaming? No. He knew it hadn't been a dream. The bottom half of the window was still open. As Pegasus had said, it was difficult to shut a window with hooves. Finn slipped out of bed and very carefully, so as to make no noise, he shut the window. As he did so, he caught sight of something unusual wrapped round the base of the little finger of his left hand. It was hair, tough and springy. Pegasus' hair. The ring that would remind him to be strong. "Will it be there in the morning?" Finn wondered as he went back to bed.

★ ★ ★ ★ ★

"What's that you've got round your finger, Finn?" his mother asked him at breakfast.

"Just some hair. If you show me how to plait it, I'm going to make it into a ring," Finn said. It was going to be awkward if she asked him how he'd got hold of a horse's hair.

"I thought you'd stopped pulling horsehair out of your mattress when you stopped being a baby," his mother said.

"I won't do it any more, Mum. But you will show me how to plait it, won't you?"

111

"All right. As long as there's enough of it. It's a funny colour, isn't it? Most horse hair that I've seen is black."

"It's silver," Finn said.

"It must have come from a very special sort of horse," his mum said.

She was right, Finn thought. Pegasus was special. He would never forget him. With the ring made from the hairs of the horse's silver mane, he would feel brave enough to face the dark tonight, and for every night to come.